Warrior Princess
Battle For The Forest

Stacey Hunter

Platinum House
Publishing

Platinum House Publishing LLC

Print Edition ISBN-13: 978-1-68096-009-9

Warrior Princess

To My Faithful Readers

ABIGALE

Abigale the forest woman grew up alone with her forest friends. But faith had sent the man that she would love stumbling into her camp, running from those fierce tribesmen.

CHAPTER ONE

******

Abigale lay still on the bed of green grasses, her hands clutched behind her beautiful blond head. She was touched by a gentle wind blowing from the south through the wide open door of the tree house, whispered of a forest long awake and very busy.

But this morning the noises from the forest held no interest for Abigale. A feeling of loneliness and sadness had gripped her from the moment she woke up.

In nearby tree tops her pet monkey, Chimp, had left his noisy pursuits since sunrise to peer anxiously in the doorway in a mistress who'd lie on such a day that was so wonderful. Also, in the clearing below, the great big elephant, Temba, stirred impatient and perplexed as the girl he looked upon as his own private pet had not appeared for the usual ceremony of eating, playing and swimming over which he often presided.

For the very first time, though, her animal friends weren't enough. The usual joy she took in lecturing, teasing and rough-housing them was gone. Even the recognizable, deep cough of the powerful, black-manned lion, Sabot, coming from across the river failed to excite Abigale.

She'd raised Sabot from a cub, and though he'd wander away for days at a time, he constantly came back, as he was doing this morning after an eight-day prowl, to dog her footsteps and cause trouble with all the other pets through his dangerous envy.

The forest girl had probed without success for some explanation of her melancholy. She knew that black men frequently were ill and for a moment she wondered if that could be her problem, though the only sickness she'd ever known was the stomach ache from eating too much unripe fruit.

She had been laid up several times with hurts suffered in life and death battles with forest beasts, but her feelings were totally different on those occasions from the way she felt now. Abigale had long beautiful blond hair and startling deep blue eyes, her full lips as amply red as rubies that are sun struck.

Her skin was soft and tanned, golden color and she had the proud, lithe carriage of a woman that is truly beautiful. And yet she had no understanding of beauty in the terms of how a civilized woman thinks of it. Abigale body was pleasing to her, yes, because in its sculptured lines and firm, supple sleekness, she recognized the same qualities she admired in the arrow-swift antelope and the great cats. But it never entered her mind as to whether she was attractive to men.

That basic feminine criterion of appearances, the male response, was a yardstick as yet unknown to Abigale, for up to now she had never known a man of her own kind. The indistinct faces of a woman and a white man occasionally had come to her in her dreams when she was younger, faces which were familiar and yet somehow beyond the reach of her memory.

Abigale's earliest memories were of the Abamas, over whom the old witch woman of the tribe, Nidi Ela, had predicted that Abigale would one day rule the forest.

To prepare her for that task, she was taken by Nidi Ela into the forest and brought her up apart from the other children as though she were a high priestess in training. But for many years now, Nidi Ela had been dead and a great, lost loneliness grew in Abigale.

Formerly, there had been no blacks in Abigale's section of the forest, for the Abamas resided five suns to the south and they continued to obey the dead witch- woman's taboo against invading Abigale's privacy. "She'll come to you when she's prepared," Nidi Ela had said. But five moons ago the warlike Bambala settled near her and had come unexpectedly from the north.

In her first encounter with them, Abigale had just escape capture. Since that time, the blacks had made sporadic attempts to hunt her down. Not wanting to cause a tribal war, Abigale had not told the Abamas of her trouble, and more recently now, the Bambala had left her alone and she'd seen that on one of those infrequent occasions when she encountered a hunter, it was the black who turned and fled.

BUT Abigale didn't think of these things as she lay on her bed of grasses. Abigale thought of little except that life was no longer exciting and good. Temba, the elephant trumpeted impatiently for her in the clearing below the tree-house.

Scarcely had the ear-splitting sounds of his summons died away when her pet monkey, scampered across the ground, Chimp, landed with a loud thump in the doorway of the house and thrust his wizened, old man's face close to hers.

Chimp chattered gently to her at first. Then, after getting no response from her, he fell silent, peered intently with his small button eyes. Chimp turned away heart-brokenly, as he plodded toward the doorway, making unhappy sounds in his throat.

"Oh, all right," Abigale muttered wearily.

"I will get up if it'll quiet you wild dingos down. By the red eyes of Gimshai, why can't you and Temba tend to your own business for one day and leave me alone?"

The forest girl spoke the rapid, musical language of the Abamas. At the sound of her voice, Chimp whirled, an almost human look of joy wreathing his black small face. He began to bounce up and down like a rubber ball, chattering with crazy animation. Abigale stood up on her feet, straightening and smoothing her halter and leopard skin shorts.

She took her sheathed knife from a wall peg, belted it on. The she picked up a bow so they rested between her shoulder blades comfortably and a full quiver of arrows. Abigale scowled at the monkey, and then with surprising animal quickness, she mimicked him exactly, even to the sound of his voice.

The monkey froze, his mouth open, his head inclined forward so that he peered at her like an old man looking over the very top of his spectacles. Then shrieking with delight, the monkey turned and whipped through the door, as if meaning to tell Temba, the elephant, of the wonderful joke.

Abigale came out on the small stage which functioned as a veranda for the tree-house. Two gold and purple virini birds whirred upward from a nearby branch to the harsh scolding of a parrot. Ten yards away in a great slanting column of sun, a group of butterflies wheeled in an endless, dizzying dance.

The forest girl looked down through the gently rocking pattern of branches to where Temba, with ponderous solemnity, was scratching his tough hide against a tree. At the side of the stage lay a coiled length of liana, one end of which was tied to a branch that was heavy.

With a sigh, Abigale nudged the rope with her foot into a space. She caught the vine with her hands, leaned over, and swung off the stage, the swift, sure agility with which she shimmied down the liana bespoke an unusual strength for a woman.

The elephant was waiting for her as her feet touched the ground. Temba looked down at her from his great height, moving his ears like mammoth fans. He then snaked his trunk about Abigale, and lifting her, swung toward the river twenty yards away.

"No, no, Temba," she protested irritably. "Let me down. I don't want to go swimming this morning."

The bull was at the water's border before he realized Abigale was in earnest. Temba set her down, peered at her with his remarkably intelligent eyes of his kind, seemingly trying to discover what was wrong.

His look gave Abigale a twinge of conscience, and trying hard to hide that fact even from herself, she turned away, stared downstream. She immediately gave an exasperated grunt. Abigale's glance had lighted on a heavy, black-maned figure carefully working its way over the river by using a low limb as a bridge.

It was Sabot, the lion, coming to start more trouble. "I'm not going to put up with it," she said fiercely. "What do these animals believe I am, a slave?"

With a toss of her chin, she started across the clearing toward the forest. She heard Temba shift his feet, she knew he was considering following her. Off to her right, Chimp the monkey came somersaulting out of a tree, landed on his feet and ran to catch her. "Leave me alone!" she hollered.

And abruptly she was running, fleeing from her forest friends as though demons chased her. She sped into the cloaking green underbrush, not giving any attention to the branches lashing her.

She ran on and on, stopping only when her breath began coming in hard gasps. When she finally stopped and composed herself, she felt ashamed and very foolish. She shook her blond head, a momentary wetness in her eyes.

What was wrong with her? Had she somehow caught the peculiar madness which sometimes came upon animals, driving them off to live in the bush alone, nursing a crazed fury against the entire forest? Abigale peeked about to get her bearings.

She hadn't paid any heed to the course she was taking and was surprised to discover how far outside her normal hunting ground she had gone. Though there certainly never had been any arrangement made between them, there was a vague line of demarcation between her own range and that of the Bamb.

The blacks themselves had more or less drawn the imaginary line in the past few months and sometimes penetrated beyond it.

Ordinarily, Abigale would have turned back instantaneously to the security of her own properties, but in her disposition today she didn't care about risk or anything else. She sat on a fallen tree and put her head in her hands. The sun crept to nearly midway in the sky before the forest girl finally got up.

A hunger pain knifed through her, reminding her she hadn't eaten all day. She was standing indecisively, when an errant breeze brought the scent of ripening fruit to her. In her life in the forest, her sense of smell had become nearly as sharp as an animal's. She went right to the stand of trees, heavy with big blue- plums.

When the taste of the plums palled, she drifted on to some nut trees and eventually topped off her effortless meal with a yellowish panyanox pear.

Abigale heard a distant, resounding roar like a small bang of thunder as she threw away the pear core. The sound was brand-new to her and she listened, frowning. Then the muted thunder came twice more, seeming to roll close along the earth.

Suddenly the forest was listening. The little rustlings in the underbrush, constant and so faint that one grew almost oblivious of them, suddenly stilled. The harsh voices of the parrots, the trilling, liquid notes of the song birds stopped in a single velvet clap of quietness. The forest listened, weighting the present danger in the alien sound.

Then as the noise blasted thrice again and still nothing happened, like a small music box starting to play, the activity of the small creatures resumes. The strange sound of thunder was ignored and then forgotten by all the animals the second it was determined it personally was not threatened.

But due to that strange, unsettled quirk in the human mind, call it a thirst for knowledge, or insatiable curiosity, or a clear contrary impulse to meddle, Abigale responded rather differently from the forest animals.

What did this new and distinct sound mean? What caused it? Could it be there was something in the forest she did not know about? Eyes glowing with interest, Abigale started running in the direction of the continuing loud noise.

She ran with elegance like an antelope, seeming to choose the easiest and the fastest route by instinct. There clearly was no likeness between Abigale's long, flashing and beautifully modeled legs' and her knock kneed, a ridiculously aimless attempt of a civilized woman to run.

In just a few minutes, she came to a wide trail burrowing like a dimly-lit tunnel through the choking growth of vines, shrubs and trees. It was one of the primeval elephant tracks which function as the highways of Africa's.

The resounding blasts were coming rapidly and closer to Abigale. Her ears picked up the sound of pounding feet, as she was about to step out on the trail.

Abigale drew back out of sight, and sensing for the very first time that she may be running into danger, she lemonkeyd high, caught a limb and drew herself up into a tree. She located a perch in the middle branches, where she commanded a clear view of the trail but would be hidden from sight herself as long as she lay flat on her stomach in a nest of vines.

A dark figure sprinted around a curve that was far in the path. A few seconds later, another two runners burst into view. Afterward an entire clot of clawing bodies came pouring with speed around the turn.

Abigale's eyes narrowed, her body suddenly tight. As the blacks swept closer along the shadowed dimness of the trail, she realized they were unusual tribesmen, not the Bambala, her enemies. The blacks were clearly terror stricken, each man fighting to get in front of the others.

None of them had the look of warriors, although the three men in the lead were equipped with shields and spears. The majority of the natives had hefty packs strapped on their backs, and as they ran, they were tearing free of the carrying straps and letting the packs shatter on the ground. Out of sight around the turn, the explosions were sounding clearer and sharper, each blast shocking the fleeing natives to greater speed.

Abigale could not picture in her mind what terror the panting, straining natives fled from. Then, suddenly, when the fleeing blacks were just a short spear throw away from either side of the trail burst forth the dread cry of the Bambala war, "Babalo Aka N'Koto!" That frenzied shout repeated over and over with shrillness that was hysterical brought back in a rush of memory to Abigale, of that ghastly

morning when they first tried capture her,
swarming out of ambush, a hundred jackals
against one unarmed woman.

But in her they'd met a raging, tearing
leopard rather than a panic- stricken victim.
And on that same day Abigale had killed for
the first time, had written in Bambala blood the
first lines of the legend of the warrior-queen
which month to month from that time on was
to grow and become greater.

"Blood for N'Koto!" Blood of the Bambala for
the evil god! Blood for that hideous, bloated
idol which the Bambala groveled, bow and
prayed before they went out to hunt down
innocent, weak victims.

Abigale snarled like an angry cat, her
beautiful, full lips shearing back to reveal bared
teeth. Out of the underbrush along the trail, the
Bambala swept in two big waves. The ambush
was planned perfectly.

At point-blank range they hammered on their
spears into their prey, ripping their swords free
from them, they charged in to finish their grisly
work.

Abigale's hand darted to her bow, as the
painted warriors fell upon the bearers that were
terrorized. All thought of her own safety was
completely gone. Red, flaming rage, seared
over her. It was but a moment's work to pull

17

loose the slip-knot holding the bow across her shoulders.

With the flashing speed and experience that comes from long practice, she snapped the bow- string tight, as though her feet rested on solid ground She lemonkeyd upright on the limb, in perfect balance.

With nerveless preciseness, the forest girl began feeding arrows into the closely packed attackers.

A Bambala warrior threw his arms up, and screaming, dropped to his knees. Another pitched forwards and was trampled underfoot. Another two fell abruptly like puppets whose strings have been cut. The fifth bent double, an arrow hammered straight through his middle, and began to run in circles like a dog with his tail on fire.

Abigale had concentrated her fire on the Bambala nearest to her, those blocking the flight of the bearers. When Abigale knocked the five men out of the uneven battle, it was like stabbing a knife into a water-filled bladder.

The distraught bearers who'd survived the first onslaught came bursting through the opening she'd created. With great speed they drove out of the snare and threw off at all angles into the great forest.

The Bambala's splintered apart, groups of four to five warriors taking out after each of the terrified human rabbits. The aggressors were fuming with rage more wildly than ever that an easy slaughter had turned into a pursuit that was difficult.

But the warriors nearest those men dropped by Abigale's arrows didn't join the pursuit. Some of them had seen the arrows rip in their fellows, and jabbering excitedly, they pointed out to the others that the attack had come from a fresh, hidden foe.

Then one of the men, stop to consider the angle at which the arrows had struck, suddenly spotted Abigale standing with her legs wide apart up on a swaying limb. He pointed his finger at the tall slim, white body drawn against the green leaves from the tree.

"Tioto Nomi!" he shouted. "The Forest Woman!"

A low, hoarse, shivering sound, like the rush of wind through a deep gorge, broke from the Bambala. There was hatred in that sound, and fear, also. This was the woman they'd hunted countless times without success.

For all their wiles, all their numbers, all their weapons, she made fools of them. Clearly, no ordinary woman would have the ability to outwit warriors. And there were other things that showed she was no ordinary flesh and blood human.

For instance, hadn't she been seen having conversation with ferocious forest animals, or hunting and playing with them. The mere woman had shown that she was immune to the curses and spells of the witch doctors, to the proven juju which will wither and kill a black man in a matter of days.

And at the same time, many happenings in the Bambala kraal, including the unseasonal windstorm two moons past which tore off the roofs of half the huts or the odd overnight invasion of snakes after the last rain, could only be attributed to the evil magic of someone like the Forest Woman.

Clearly, without a doubt, the mere woman was the spawn of demons, devils that are endowed with a strong personal juju, else the forest devils themselves would long ago have devoured her.

Fear does different things to various men. Most of the warriors were paralyzed for a brief moment, astonished by the knowledge that Abigale for the first time had attacked them and invaded their lands. But one squat, bull-chested native was galvanized into action.

"Quick, Save yourselves!" he yelled. "Attack before she kills us!"

He pulled on a spear from one of the dead warriors body, his eyes inflated, his mouth a hard, wide open hole. With rage, he ran forward two steps, raising the spear for the cast.

CHAPTER TWO

******

bigale's arrow took the spear-man in the throat, threw him flopping backwards like a beheaded chicken. But, the action of the man broke the spell which held the other Bambala warriors.

They went scrambling for spears among the bearers that were dead. Swift as she was, Abigale did not have enough time to escape, and against a massed spear strike she couldn't be saved by her bow.

Too late she now realized she had been betrayed by her deep seated hatred of the Bambala into recklessness that was deadly.

Then, at that moment, as death swiftly reached for her, three men came quickly around the far turn of the trail behind the angry warriors. Two of them were big and strong blacks wearing bleached khaki shorts.

The husky men clutched rifles in their large hands, almost empty cartridge belts hitting their waistlines as they ran.

The third man was a tall, broad shouldered white man with the driving, high stepping pace of a football fullback. He gripped a rifle in his hands, a pistol belted about his midsection that was slender.

He was not wearing a hat, his black hair unruly and tangled. And though exhaustion and strain lined his square-jawed face, giving him at first glance a deceptive look of maturity, a more searching inspection told he was in his early twenties.

The two black men hesitated, broke stride, when they saw the Bambala milling among the dying and dead bearers. Both of them, eyes suddenly gleaming white, cast frightened glances over their shoulders.

The white man's voice lashed them, drove them on a few slowing steps further out. But the same panic that had overtaken the bearers was fountaining up in the two guards.

As though they had been snared by invisible ropes, the guards stopped, making useless little twists and turns, without ever actually moving from their tracks, the white man's husky voice whipped them again, this time with angry urgency in it.

One of them shook his head violently, saying he wouldn't charge the Bambala. The other gave no sign he even heard. The husky white man hesitated for a few seconds, then his mouth twisting bitterly, he rushed forward alone, triggering his rifle from hip-level as he ran.

His shouts to the guards had shuddered the Bambala warriors' attention away from Abigale. They gave cry like a dog pack when they saw the three new victims. Two of them, spears lifting very high, leaped to meet with the oncoming white man.

Then the white man's rifle was jerking and bucking in his rigidly straining hands. At that range even not even un-aimed shots could not miss. The crash of the explosions echoed and reechoed, sound stacking on sound, in the cavern-like trail.

At that moment, one of the charging spear-men seemed to run into a stone wall. In mid-stride he slammed against the unseen barrier, went reeling back in a twisting fall.

By the time he hit the ground, two more men in the group of natives behind him were going down and a third was crying with a shattered arm. These warriors were, hard-bitten and tough, but this was their first encounter in facing gunfire. That terrible roaring fire stick was awesome to watch, as a herd of charging elephants.

Dreadful magic was in a weapon which in, some mysterious way spat death through the air.

And the best measure of the fire stick's magic was the way the lone white man ran directly towards them.

Only a strong and brave man who knew he could not lose this battle would fling himself against overwhelming odds. Flesh and blood couldn't fight the magic of that fire stick. The Bambala didn't guess the colossal bluff the white man was running on them.

It took iron courage to drive at those blacks, triggering the last of his rifle cartridges, realizing he was finished if they didn't break before he reached them.

It wasn't lunatic bravery that dictated his action. The forest behind him was alive with Bambala. The main force had attacked his safari from the rear, overwhelming over half the bearers before he could bring his guns into play, stampeding the rest into this second ambush.

He knew he wouldn't have a chance against the forest-wise blacks if he turned off into the underbrush. The trail ahead offered the only avenue of flight.

He had seen in the first moments of battle that the warriors were gun shy. By fighting a fierce rearguard action, he and the two armed blacks had tried to buy time for the bearers to escape. But when their ammunition ran low, they, too, had been forced to run for it. Thinking of their nearly empty rifles, the guards' nerves had broken when they rounded the turn and saw their retreat cut off.

The white man had gritted his teeth and plowed on. He had kept his wits enough to realize that a bold front might panic the small group of natives blocking the path.

And if his bluff failed?

Well, he would only be dying a few seconds sooner than the two fear-stricken guards.

But his bluff didn't fail. Like jackals charged by a lion, the Bambala suddenly took to their heels. In a trampling rush, they headed into the underbrush, leaving the path clear.

Abigale stood frozen on the limb above the trail. She was as startled by that thundering fire stick as the natives, but she was even more stunned by the fact that the fire stick's master was white-skinned. She didn't fear him. After all, he had saved her life. His reckless charge had turned the Bambala spears away from her in the nick of time.

It didn't occur to her that he could be anything but a friend and ally. She judged men by the only rule stick she knew, the ways of the animal world. Among the forest creatures, like ran with like, instinctively sharing the same hatreds, hungers, and habits.

Early in life, Abigale reluctantly had concluded that she was a creature alone, doomed to spend her days without ever knowing the company of others like herself.

And now suddenly, unbelievably, she was seeing one of her own people—a male of her own kind! That he was a male, she had no doubt. His square-jawed face, his broad shoulders, deep chest and lean hips, his deep voice and wild, fierce manner of fighting, all bespoke his maleness.

He braked to a stop almost directly beneath her, and swung about, hands busy with the fire stick. The thing that had stopped the white man was the hideous up thrust of Bambala cries on the trail behind him. As he turned, fumbling in haste to jam the last of his cartridges into the rifle, he saw black warriors pouring around the turn and washing out of the forest on both sides of the two guards who had lagged behind him.

He jerked the rifle up, slammed five purposeful shots into the swarming mass. But a score of marksmen could not have saved the two men. The Bambala were on them like craving animals, ripping the guards to bits with their hands.

As the clawing, howling mass closed over the two, the white man's finger reflexively kept working the gun trigger.

But the five shells had been his last and the hammer snapped unsuccessfully against an empty chamber.

His right hand snaked for his pistol, his clean cut face gone white with anger under his deep suntanned skin, when he finally realized what he was doing. Then with the pistol half outside of its holster, he came to his senses, realizing the pointlessness of attempting to contest that overpowering force.

He turned abruptly, and still holding tight the empty rifle, went thumping down the track. His action broke the strong spell which had held Abigale motionless.

She had seen him feed five glittering metal
tubes into the fire stick, had heard it spit
thunder five times and then emit only empty
clicks. The five ejected cartridges lay on the trail
where he had stood.

Her quick mind fitted these facts together
and suddenly she realized the fire stick's magic
was used up. The Bambala, already starting the
pursuit, soon would also realize the gun's
magic was exhausted. And once the caution
engendered by their fear of that gun was gone,
they would make short work of the white man.

"Oh, no!" exclaimed Abigale aloud. "I can't let
them get him!"

With flying fingers, she dropped the arrow
she held back into the quiver, secured the bow
on her back. Then with the sure agility of one of
the tree people themselves, she started through
the middle branches. It was through this trick
of tree travel that she had so many times
mystified the Bambala, apparently vanishing
into thin air just when they thought they had
her cornered.

As a lonesome child, she had begun imitating
the monkeys and apes as strictly a matter of
play, and through endless practice gradually

she had become breathtakingly expert at aerial acrobatics.

In pursuing the white man, Abigale veered off to the left through the forest, remembering that the trail made a leisurely arc. Despite his considerable lead on her, she would be able to intercept him by making the shortcut.

When she reached her destination, she saw him a hundred yards away, coming fast towards her. The Bambala weren't in sight yet, but the clearness with which their chilling cries could be heard told that they weren't far behind.

Abigale gripped a dangling length of liana, balanced to swing down onto the trail. And then, with the actual moment of meeting this strange male at hand, the forest girl was gripped by an overpowering shyness.

She could hear her heart pounding rapidly, the swift rise and fall of her breast, and in the pit of her belly as well as her legs, she had an unusual, feeling that was quaky. The forest girl hesitated, bewildered by these surprising and totally new sensations.

Then angrily, she told herself, "You fool, do not cling in this tree like a scared lizard while death races up on that courageous man."

And with that, she leaped clear of the limb, went swinging down onto the trail. Just before

her feet touched the ground, she turned loose of
the vine and hit running. As the man saw a
figure hurtle out of the tree, he came to a
sliding stop, tearing his pistol from its holster.
His eyes flew wide as Abigale hit the trail, took
three long running steps and halted, facing
him. His gun arm seemed to wilt, slowly
dropping back to his side.

"Good lord!" he said quite audibly. "A white
girl!"

Abigale heard his startled exclamation, and
though she didn't understand the words, the
sound of his voice was pleasant to her. She saw
too that her appearance had greatly confused
and upset him. She couldn't know that in
addition to his shock at finding a white girl in
the midst of nowhere, he was suddenly frantic
with the thought that the responsibility for her
life was being placed in his hands when he
couldn't hope to take care of himself.

His face was tragic as he stared at her fresh,
young beauty. In his mental turmoil, details
such as her unusual dress or the odd manner in
which she had appeared didn't immediately
make an impression on him.

His mind was too filled with the horror of the
Bambala attack for him to think logically. She

was the most beautiful girl he had ever seen
and it sickened him to realize he was helpless to
protect her from the murderous blacks.

Then the girl was beckoning to him, dire
urgency in her gesture. He dropped the pistol
back into his holster. He saw by her manner
that she was thoroughly aware of the pursuing
blacks, but she didn't show the least sign of
fear.

He tried to frame what he should say to her,
wondering whether to tell her right out how
scant were their chances or whether to lull her
with a false sense of security.

But before he could speak, she ran forward
impatiently and caught him by the hand. For
the merest instant, her blue eyes stared directly
into his gray ones, seeming in their electric
intensity to search deep within him. She turned
then, and gripping his hand with surprising
strength, tugged him into a run.

She kept a step ahead of him and he could no
longer escape seeing the bow and quiver of
arrows tied across her shoulders. He frowned,
his mind struggling sluggishly with the fact
that the bow was polished by long usage; the
primitive doeskin quiver worn with much
handling, His glance went to the long knife
riding the curve of her hip, noted that the ivory

handle was shaped for a woman's grip instead of a black warrior's broad, thick fingers.

And abruptly, a host of disturbing details about her began to drop into place.

He felt the strength of her strong grip on his arm, watched the lithe play of her firm muscles underneath her velvety beautiful skin, saw the golden suntan which covered her slender body.

He noticed that she was wearing her leopard skin clothing, which though worked to a beautiful softness, was yet cut and sewn crudely.

Her feet were bare and she wore not one ornament. From the first couple of steps he took in following her, he could sense she was not leading him in blind flight. There was a confidence in her movements that assured him she had a clear plan figured out.

This was not what he'd anticipated. Instead of being a frightened woman seeking protection, she had taken serene command of their escape.

She swerved to the right into what appeared to the white man an impenetrable wall of vegetating and directed him some fifty yards down the elephant trail.

But she wriggled with sure speed through the vine-choked bush, turning and twisting right and left as if by instinct to find clearance.

Twenty paces off the main trail he had lost all sense of direction.

He discovered that the going was easier and found that she had brought them to a miniature, winding game path way. She turned loose of his hand and began to sprint along the narrow pathway like a doe that was running.

Green branches slashed at his face, caught at his rifle as he tried to keep up with her. Roots caught his booted feet and the green tall bushes gripped his legs. He felt like a blind bull threshing through the forest, as he saw how easily she threaded through the undergrowth ahead of him, he got angry with himself. The white man strained to the outermost limits of his strength to stay up with her.

His legs grew unsteady and his straining lungs ached with effort. Perspiration poured from him in a drenching flood. And to add to his humiliation in being not able to match the girl, he fell sprawling full length in the path and stumbled over the roots of a baobab tree.

With the breath knocked out of him, He was too weak for a moment even to get to his knees again. When he lifted his head, he saw the forest girl had turned back and was staring down at him with a questioning look on her face.

He growled sheepishly and said, "I am all right." "These blasted boots are not easy to run in."

The blond girl cocked her head at his words, but did not say a word. He realized that she hadn't spoken a word the entire time, and suddenly wondered why. He got on his feet and gave her a friendly grin. He did not want her to think of him ungrateful.

His weak grin immediately brought an answering smile from her.

She gestured to him to get started, and as if to reinforce her warning that he must keep running, the savage howls of their pursuers rose along their back trail. He saw how swiftly the sound of the pack erased her smile and knew the Bambala were dangerously close. His own features sobered.

"Go on," he said, motioning her ahead.

"You mustn't lag back because I'm so damnably slow.

By yourself you can outrun them for sure.

Forget about me and let me make out for myself."

Abigale studied him thoughtfully, puzzling out his meaning. Then setting her lips firmly, she marched forward and caught him by the arm It was obvious she had no intention of leaving him.

"Ohhh," he said despairingly, "all right, I'll go. You'd stand here until they ran over us. But you're being plain foolish."

She started off again, this time adjusting her pace to his ability to stay up with her. It angered him to realize this, to appear a flabby weakling in her eyes, and he drove himself unmercifully in an effort to crowd her, but always she kept the same distance ahead of him, seeming to float effortlessly along the difficult path.

He did his best, but it wasn't good enough. The measure of his inadequacy was the growing speed with which the Bambala began to overtake them. But lacking Abigale animal-keen hearing, he didn't realize how desperately close a handful of the swifter blacks had come behind them.

Abigale knew that these warriors, the best runners of the tribe, had long since outdistanced the pack. Only the confused winding of the path concealed them from view; otherwise, they would have been in easy arrow range.

She had doubled back onto the trail she had followed in first entering the Bambala area, hoping that once she crossed the vaguely defined border between her lands and theirs that they would abandon the chase.

But she had failed to take into consideration the white man's difficulty in following her through the bush.

Because of his slowness, the blacks had cut away their lead. The Bambala could tell from the white man's spoor that he was staggering with exhaustion.

With their prey almost in their grasp, the frenzy of the chase submerged their hazy fears of Abigale. They plunged across the border without hesitation, confident they could make a quick and easy kill and get back to their own lands before any harm could come to them.

When the warriors failed to turn back, a sudden chill touched Abigale heart. The man was doomed. Despite all she could do, this black-haired, fair-skinned male of her own kind would be slain.

It would still be an easy matter for her to get away from the Bambala. But all her forest cunning was useless to help this man. She heard him reel and clutch at a tree for support.

She stopped, turned back. His head was dropped forward on his chest, his face

contorted with the struggle to breathe. He
sagged against the tree for a moment, looking
as though his legs were going to give under
him. Then through the wetness of his shirt she
saw his back and shoulder muscles tense and
he shoved himself away from the tree, came
weaving toward her.

She sensed the effort of will behind that
action.

Her blue eyes were dark with the decision
she made.

She put out her arms and halted him.

He swayed under the suddenness of her grip,
then slowly she stepped away from him,
staring bleakly along the way the Bambala
would come. He wheeled about, watching her
as she reached for her bow.

Abruptly, understanding came to him. This
strange, magnificent girl, rather than abandon
him to his fate, was preparing to face their
pursuers with no other weapon than her
primitive bow.

The hoarse protest that burst from his lips
was drowned by a lion's ear- splitting roar.
Before his amazed eyes, a huge, black-maned
lion burst from a stand of shoulder-high grass
to crouch facing them in the path. The beast
was a giant of his kind, a steel-thewed male in

his very prime, his narrowed, yellow eyes blazing with deadliness.

For the merest fraction of time, the white man was shocked into immobility. It was as though a searing electric current stabbed into him from the cat's yellow eyes. Then with a wild, warning yell to the girl, his right hand dove for his pistol.

CHAPTER THREE

✳✳✳✳✳✳

B OB knew as he went for the gun how small a chance he had of stopping the lion. But his instinct was to protect the girl, and if nothing else, the shots would draw the brute's charge to him.

Suddenly, bewilderingly, the blond girl plunged at him, fought his hand away from the pistol.

A part of his mind dazedly registered the fact that she was screaming at him in the Abama tongue, not English. He understood the words easily for he had just come from a long stay with the Nubutus, blood cousins of the Abamas, who lived a month's trek to the west.

"No, no!" she said. "Don't harm Sabot! He's my friend! I can control him."

He thought either he had gone crazy or he was dreaming the granddaddy of all nightmares. Over the girl's shoulder he could see the cat slink forward in slow, crouching steps, the unblinking eyes riveted on his face.

The realization came to him that the lion was making no effort to charge the easy target made by the girl's back, but was holding back, waiting with coiled muscles for her to move out of the way.

He was the one the lion was after, not the girl!

The girl had wrestled him back against a tree. It was suddenly all too much for the confused, bone-weary man. He quit struggling for the gun, sagged back against the rough bark.

At that moment, he no longer cared whether he lived or died. As soon as he relaxed, the girl spun around to face the black maned cat.

Keeping between the man and the slowly approaching beast, she began to talk in a calm, firm voice. The lion's ears shifted to catch her words, and after an interval, his glance flicked from the man to the girl.

When she had the cat looking at her, Abigale went up to him. The lion allowed her to stroke him, the deep-throated snarls changing in tone, becoming complaining rather than chilling.

She scratched him behind an ear, slid her arm about his neck, and with gradual pressure, turned the giant cat completely about on the trail. Still keeping her arm around the brute's shaggy mane, she began to walk, leading him away from the man.

Before she had gone five steps, the first of the pursuing blacks burst into view on the trail. The warrior rounded a turn at a terrific pace.

The native had abandoned his spear to achieve greater speed, feeling his sword and bow were weapons enough to handle the two whites. He leaned forward as he ran, arms pumping, eyes glued to the trail.

Abigale stabbed a hand toward the warrior, pygmy words spilling from her lips. The huge lion beside her stiffened, his great head lifting.

Abruptly, the cat's tail lashed, a tremendous roar smashed from his throat. Then with the blinding speed of a thunderbolt, he shot down the trail toward the warrior.

The Black's head jerked up as he heard the roar. His eyes seemed to triple in size, his face blanching a dirty gray. With a wild flailing of arms and legs, he managed to whip around and start back toward the turn.

But at that moment, five more warriors running in single file sprinted into view. The fleeing black hammered into the line of his fellows, screaming, "Simba, Simba!" and clawing for his sword.

His cry of "Lion, Lion!" was no warning. All he succeeded in doing was to send the first three men sprawling over him in a confused tangle. The last two blacks did manage to keep their feet, skidding to a stop just in time to make perfect targets for the charging lion.

Abigale savage pet shot completely over the fallen men and landed with demoniac fury on the rear two warriors.

Sabot's tearing claws and fangs had ripped the blacks to shreds before he had borne them to the ground.

The great lion wasted no time on his first victims.

Barely had his feet touched earth when he reared about and dove directly on the fallen mass of men.

He seemed to understand that he must strike before the warriors could bring their weapons into play. The watching white man was never to forget that awful scene.

The natives screams cut through the bloodcurdling snarls of the maddened cat. The black- maned brute was all over, spinning, twisting, leaping, and striking down the scared warriors before they could flee.

And suddenly it was over and the bloodstained lion stood among the torn things that had once been men and cried his kingly rage to the forest. His one loyalty was to Abigale.

Baring his fangs and tossing his head, he roared defiance at all those who would harm her. The white man rubbed a hand across his eyes, muttered, "—unbelievable—that devil obeying her—fighting for her—" But it was only the first of the astonishing experiences in store for him.

The girl's whole being had changed. Her eyes blazed with excitement. She was no longer a person resigned to death. She ran up to him, momentarily forgetting that he had spoken in a strange tongue.

"Come!" she said exultantly in Abama.
"They'll never catch us now! Temba is bound to be close by.

Nothing but jealousy would have made Sabot follow me this distance. He was afraid Temba would get me off to himself and he'd go to any lengths to keep that from happening." "I don't know who or what you're talking about," he answered hoarsely, "but I darn sure don't want to stay here with that lion."

She was pulling him down the path then, her darting eyes searching the forest about them.

It was a full minute before she realized that, except for a few strange words like "darn," he had replied to her in the Abama language. She looked at him, a smile like a burst of sunlight curving her full lips.

"You do speak as I do," she said happily. "My heart sank when first I heard you speak in a strange tongue, for I thought you were different from me. But we are the same—the same skin, the same language, the same blood."

Uneasy wonder at the mystery of this strange forest girl stirred the white man again. She had the beauty of a goddess, the ways of a wild creature. She was undoubtedly white, but spoke Abama as her native language and seemed to have no knowledge of her own race at all.

And this Temba she spoke of, who was he? Another lion? Or was he some hulking brute of a wild man.

The thought of her belonging to some man hadn't occurred to him before. He found he was oddly disturbed.

"Are you sure this Temba person will welcome me?" he asked.

"Temba?" she said, surprised. "He won't mind."

The white man wet his lips. "Uh—is he your husband?" He had to ask it. She repeated the Abama word for husband under her breath as though she were unsure she had heard him aright. Then suddenly a peal of delighted laughter burst from her throat.

"Oh, no," she said, her voice husky with laughter.

"The sly old lazybones has practically moved in with me and thinks he owns me, but he's hardly the type for a husband."

The white man nervously cleared his throat, his face grown more somber than ever. He failed to see any humor in the situation. It was only further proof, he told himself, of how desperately little he really knew about women.

He stared darkly at the ground, the trees, the leaf-obscured sky, anywhere so he wouldn't have to look into those dancing blue eyes. A damnable crime, he boiled silently. A young and beautiful girl like that.

Looked like the picture of innocence, too. Another tragedy of environment, but probably it was far too late to do anything about it now.

Her glad cry broke into his thoughts. "There he is! There's Temba! I knew he wouldn't be far away."

He looked grimly in the direction she pointed. For a moment, since he was prepared to see a man, his glance registered nothing but green shrubs with a huge, gray, rock-like mound vaguely visible behind them.

Then the mound moved, shoved through the undergrowth with amazing speed and quiet toward the girl, and with astonished eyes he recognized a mammoth elephant.

"That is Temba?" he sputtered. His face reddened as he became aware of her laughing regard.

"We must hurry," she said, grown suddenly serious. "The Bambala will be slowed down by the sight of those bodies and Sabot may pick off another one or two, but so long as they have a spoor to follow they'll stay after us." The elephant had stopped a few paces away and was regarding her with first one keen little eye and then the other.

"Here Temba, lift him up," she commanded.

The white man retreated a step.

"He won't hurt you," she said in an aside.

She reached out and patted the man on the shoulder for the elephant's benefit.

"I don't feel like I can move," he said tensely, "but if it is all the same to you I'll take walking rather than this." He took another backward step away from the forest giant. She beamed for the elephant, and said in a whisper, "Don't be foolish.

He's as gentle as a baby rabbit."

"Well, why are you whispering then?" the man demanded.

"I don't want him to get the idea you're afraid," she declared. "He might not respect you."

"Oh, great!" he said.

But when she gave him that pleading look, he suddenly found himself standing firmly while the Grey giant approached, suspiciously investigated him with his Hugh trunk.

He immediately thought of a burly policeman efficiently playing a sketchy character. Perhaps it was his imagination, but Temba gave Abigale a rather angry look also.

"Hurry up, Temba," snapped Abigale, "I'll explain everything to you later."

The next thing the man knew, the elephant's trunk had snapped gently but securely about his waist and he was being swept high in the air. By the time he had scrambled to a safe perch on Temba's back Abigale was settling herself on the broad head, slipping her long, shapely legs down behind the beast's ears.

She drummed her heels, spoke a quick command, and the elephant turned and went at a surprisingly fast gait down the path. The girl sat the forest giant as though she were glued on, but the man jounced, slipped and slid all over the swaying back.

His first experience with the ancient art of elephant riding couldn't be termed a successful one.

For what seemed an eternity, he struggled to stay on that lurching back.

He was too busy trying with only two hands to hold onto his rifle, clutch the rough, loose skin and block out the branches that lashed at him with diabolical aim to pay any attention to where they were headed. When Temba did stop, the white man's head was whirling dizzily in one direction, his stomach in another.

The soft, little clucking sounds of sympathy Abigale made as she helped him climb down touched his masculine pride. "Isn't this a fine thing," he told himself angrily. "Here I am acting like a maiden great-aunt, and she's as fresh and strong as when this nightmare started."

She solicitously maneuvered him to where he could sit down and rest his back against the tree trunk. He felt almost as bad as he had once when he was sea- sick and he sat with his eyes closed until she suddenly was holding a gourd of cold water to his lips.

He took a few cautious sips of the water and used the rest to bathe his face. He immediately felt better. He lifted his head to thank her.

A small black face with brilliant, glittering black eyes hung upside down in the air not four inches from his own startled features.

"Ugh!" he exclaimed and slammed himself back against the tree.

"Oh, I'm sorry," apologized Abigale. "It's only Chimp. He wanted to get a good look at you."

And shame-facedly, the man realized the strange apparition was nothing more than a small monkey hanging from a limb by his feet. He looked about at the pleasant, tree-shaded clearing, the tree-house high above him, the cool, clear deeps of the river.

"You live here?" he asked unbelievingly. "And all alone?"

She nodded enthusiastically.

Chimp, apparently tiring at long last of his upside down position, loosened his grip on the limb, turned a quick flip and landed in a squatting position in the white man's lap.

"I can't imagine how you manage," he said, trying not to notice the monkey's stern, unblinking scrutiny. "How long have you lived this way?"

"Why, always," she said matter-of-factly. "Doesn't everyone live about the same way? Of course, I do live in a tree-house, whereas most natives build on the ground.

There's plenty of game and plenty of water here. I don't think anyone could find a more perfect home."

He thought of the great crowded cities of America, the unnumbered kinds of stores,

services and establishments, the huge
manufacturing plants, the giant utilities, the
layers upon layers of governing bodies.

And this slim, wide- eyed, blond girl asked
him if everyone didn't live about the same way
she did. An existence such as hers, let alone a
happy, healthful existence, had become
inconceivable to the white races of the world.

"Surely, you remember your family," he
ventured.

A shadow seemed to pass across her face.
"No," she said.
"They died while I was a baby.
The Abamas found me, but they can tell me
nothing except that my parents were of the
Tribe of God." The expression was one used by
natives to describe white missionaries.
Grown suddenly moody, she bit her full
lower lip, stared off across the river. A wave of
sympathy swept over the man. But the girl's
mood swiftly passed. She turned back to him,
as bright and vivacious as ever.

"You haven't told me how you are called,"
she said shyly.

"Great Scot," he exclaimed in English, "I really am the boy for manners."

She blinked at him. "That is your name?"

He laughed. "No, no. My name is Bob Reilly."

She pronounced it after him cautiously, like a child learning a new phrase. Then as if she had made a startling discovery, she asked, "Why do you have two names?" Without thinking, he returned, "Why not? Most people have three."

She looked troubled.

"I have only one—Abigale," she confessed in a disturbed whisper. "I guess it is a bad thing to have only one name?" It dawned on him that she wasn't joking.

In her first tentative brush with civilization, he was unwittingly making her feel certain "lacks" in herself. He sought to reassure her.

"The main reason for a name is so you'll be known and remembered," he said. "As lovely a girl as you doesn't need more than one name.

There would never be a chance of your being confused with any other girl. No matter how many Abigale there were in the world, once a man saw you, the name Abigale would never mean anyone but you."

She gravely considered his words. It was the first male compliment she had ever received. It hadn't occurred to her that how she looked might have any effect on a man. She pursed her lips, trying to figure out his exact meaning.

"You mean," she picked her words slowly, "that you find it good to look upon me?"

Bob Reilly went through a considerable process of throat clearing. He should have remembered that women were quite unable to view any matter in the abstract. They dealt with everything on a purely personal basis.

He noticed how she leaned her head forward and frowningly looked herself over as though wondering what there could be that was particularly pleasing about her.

"Anyone would say that you are unusually beautiful," he said with enforced calm. There, he had avoided the personal angle quite neatly. She smiled. You could see the pleasure grow in her.

"I—I feel quite different," she said, "from your saying that."

He found himself watching her apprehensively, and it was with a distinct sense of relief that he saw her turn away, walk to the river bank and lean over to study her reflection.

The monkey still squatted in his lap. He hadn't thought one of the little varmints could stay quiet so long. Maybe the frozen-faced devil was trying to hypnotize him.

Bob stole a glance at Abigale, and certain she wasn't watching him, he made the most vicious, menacing face he could at the monkey.

Chimp registered absolutely no reaction. He didn't turn a hair.

Bob lifted his hands to his ears and waggled them in the universally insulting gesture of brattish children. Chimp's hard little eyes didn't so much as move. Bob bared his teeth, made ugly croaking sounds deep in his throat.

Then with insulting slowness, the monkey raised his own hands to his cars, twisted his black little features into a leering grimace, and mimicked the man's gestures with a brazen exactitude.

When he had finished, Chimp made a sound suspiciously like a horse laugh, leaped to the ground and went skittering off across the clearing in high good humor.

CHAPTER FOUR

******

BOB leaned back against the tree and closed his eyes. Too much had happened to him in too short a time.

"If I don't pull myself together," he told himself, "I'll be going off my trolley permanently."

His conscience was hurting him because he was deliberately pushing away thoughts of the ambush and of what his next move must be.

But he realized he was too confused and beat up to plan logically.

The son of one of America's wealthiest men, Bob at twenty-three, with a hat full of scholastic and sports honors and an eagerness to get out and prove himself in the world, had found himself faced with even more sterile, needless years of study.

His stepmother, as a means of getting him out from underfoot, had convinced his father it would be well to send him abroad for advanced schooling.

And the long obedient Bob eventually rebelled. In an unpleasant scene with his angry, desk-thumping dad and stepmother that was scornful, he steadfastly declared his independence, and ended by storming out of the house in a white fury.

Imbued with a need to escape from everything representing his old life, he remembered an expedition being organized by one of his previous professors to study and record indigenous African languages.

He'd shown an uncommon aptitude for that languages in school, as well as that talent of his scholarship and overall record of the publicity significance of his name, made it much easier for him to get on the expedition as a junior assistant.

After three months in the bush, the elderly professor's health broke down and he had to return home, leaving Bob in charge.

If anything, the work went better under the younger man's direction, and he began to feel he was going to show his father that he wasn't the only Reilly who could pull his own weight under difficult circumstances.

But his desire to include the more primitive and little-known tribes in his study drew him into the trackless depths of unexplored territory. He had known there was danger and had taken what he considered were adequate steps to protect his safari.

But in his inexperience, he failed to realize the vast difference between the fighting qualities of his long subjugated coastal blacks and those of the fierce, marauding tribesmen of the interior.

His guards and bearers were boastful enough about their fighting prowess until trouble came. Then they fled in panic, abandoning both packs and weapons. And so Bob's attempt to stand on his own feet, to do something striking enough to impress his father, ended in utter disaster.

"I've botched the whole thing," he told himself. "I'm a failure. No expedition will give me a chance after this, and now my parents will expect me to come crawling back to them.

And I'll have the blood of those murdered men on my hands the rest of my life." It was these torturing thoughts that Bob tried to push away from him as he sat in Abigale clearing.

At last his very weariness came to his rescue. His chin dropped forward on his chest and he slid away into a deep sleep.

Night had fallen when Bob awakened. A great silver moon lay low in the sky. The moonlight washed the river with beauty, painted shifting patterns on the ground beneath the tall trees.

The weird night chorus of the forest rose all about the clearing. Bob sat up in alarm, unable at first to identify his surroundings. A fire, burned down to red coals, glowed in the center of the clearing. He smelled the savory scent of a joint of meat grilling slowly over the fire.

"Where the devil am I?" he muttered, hurriedly reassuring himself that his pistol was still in its holster.

It was silent, there was no movements in the clearing. It looked utterly empty.

Then his glance caught on a dark bulk hunched not thirty feet from him in the shadow of a tree trunk.

He waited and took a moment to catch his breath. Suddenly the dark bulk moved, and then, two slanting yellow eyes stare at him wickedly from the shadows.

There lay a Hugh cat crouched there, watching him!

The sight of the cat swept cobwebs from his brain. He recalled Abigale and her savage pet. If she had wandered off and left him alone with that animal, he wouldn't have a chance. He felt cold sweat dripping down his face.

What should he do? If he moved or called out, that beast might charge. He remembered the stories he had read about intrepid hunters playing dead when through some accident they'd found themselves at the mercy of a lion.

But as he thought of these storybook heroes, he saw Sabot flatten himself on the ground, creep forwards a good two-feet on his belly. He did not feel the least bit intrepid at that moment.

"ABIGALE!" he called loudly. "ABIGALE!"

"Here I am." Her voice came from the direction of the river. "What's wrong?"

"Get this blasted lion of yours away from me! He's ready to spring."

"Oh, is that all," she said, obviously relieved. "Don't worry about Sabot. He wouldn't hurt you now for the world."

At the sound of his mistress' voice, Sabot stood up and looked toward the river. The instant those yellow eyes were off of him, Bob was up and around behind the tree against which he had been leaning. Once out of sight of the cat, he streaked for another tree, further away.

When he reached it safely, he began to work his way toward the water with all the care of an infantryman under heavy fire.

He reached the bank muttering. A hasty glance over the moon-swept water failed to reveal any sign of her.

He looked over his shoulder. Sabot was moving toward him with slow steps, pausing every few feet to sniff the night air.

Bob turned back toward the river just in time to see Abigale head break the surface of the water. Of all the cold-blooded women, he thought. She amuses herself by swimming around under water while her man-killing pet stalks me.

She saw him in the moonlight. "I was beginning to think you never would wake up," she said. "Come on in the water. It feels wonderful.

The meal won't be ready for awhile yet anyway." With Sabot stalking him, there was no room in Bob's mind for the proprieties in nothing flat, he had tugged off his boots and stripped to his shorts.

Cats, even big cats, didn't like water. He would be safe in the river.

Bob took two running steps and drove out over the water in a racing dive. He drove out toward mid-stream with a smooth powerful stroke, leaving a frothing wake. "How swiftly you go," she exclaimed as he swam up to her.

"Like the finny ones themselves! Oh, if only I could swim that way! I've studied every animal I could, trying to learn better ways of swimming, but none of them can match you."

He had meant to lecture to her about Sabot. But he found himself saying almost moderately, "You've got to do something about that lion. Didn't you realize he was creeping up to kill me?" "Faugh," she said mildly. "On the trail— yes—he would have killed you.

But now he understands you're my friend. He's been lying there looking at you since long before dark. After all, he never saw a white man before and he's kind of interested."

"I tell you he even came creeping after me down to the river," insisted Bob. "I don't like him and he doesn't like me." Abigale laughed. Back on the shore the black-maned lion coughed petulantly.

Both the girl and the man looked in his direction. He stood there with his head held high, gazing out at them over the water.

"Oh Well, Sabot probably thinks we would be better off without you," she confessed, "but I told him you belonged to me and to leave you alone. And he'll do it!"

Bob's mind had stopped dead on the words, "I told him you belonged to me." Bob was abruptly perplexed.

What was going on in the head of this young and wild girl that was pagan? The next thing he knew she was swimming so close to him that he could feel the touch of her naked leg against his as she treaded the water.

"I have been thinking about what you said to me this afternoon," she suddenly declared. Her eyes were disturbingly large and luminous in the moonlight.

"What was that?" he asked.

"About you finding me attractive," she explained. "That made me very happy. I could not really understand what you meant at first," Abigale went on. "I have never been around any men of my own kind, so it hadn't occurred to me that--well--that they might like me or not like me." "Yes. Quite so," Bob said uneasily.

"Don't you think you should look at the food?" Abigale face was immediately sympathetic. "Oh, I forgot," she said. "I am not used to having visitors. You must be starving.

Before he could move, she stood up and thrust her feet against the river floor.

He realized for the very first time that she swam unclad and her unexpectedly revealed beauty made his breath catch in his throat.

Abigale's naked body was an image of Aphrodite rising from the ocean. She waded to the bank. With a child-like innocence, she stood there smoothing the glistening globules of water from her body with her hands.

After leisurely donning her halter and shorts, she walked across to the fire, scrutinized the joint of meat cooking over the crossbars.

Bob dressed in the shadow of a tree in a hurry, when she called him to join her near the fire to eat. The food was very delicious and he ate an enormous amount of it, even though he had no idea what he was eating.

Never in his life had Bob felt such conflicting emotions about anyone as he did about the forest girl.

He kept stealing glimpses at Abigale while she sat cross legged beside him, eating with unconcealed enjoyment, or as she moved back and forth from the fire, waiting on him.

Abigale beamed with happiness.

And suddenly he realized that he was happy also. By all rights, he felt he should have been wallowing in the depths of despair.

He was lost in the depths of an untracked forest, hunted by murderous tribesmen, left with no adequate means of shielding himself. Yet never had he felt so vibrantly alive as he did now.

CHAPTER FIVE

✶✶✶✶✶✶

The raucous argument of parrots on a limb above him awakened Bob in the morning. He had slept near the fire, using a zebra skin thrown over freshly-cut grasses for his bed.

The moment he sat up, his eyes went to the tree house high above him. He realized that his first thoughts were of the blond-haired girl. "This won't do," he warned himself.

"I'm supposed to be a serious, intelligent adult."

He got up and began to pace the clearing, forcing everything out of his mind but his wrecked expedition. He had to decide what to do.

He could be a quitter, write off the expedition as a total loss and concentrate on trying to get out of this scrape with his own skin whole. Under the circumstances, that didn't seem too illogical.

But Bob kept remembering that a good part of the records of the expedition were in those packs abandoned by the bearers. The Bambala were certain to gather up the packs, cart them back to their village as loot.

Until he knew those records were definitely destroyed, he felt bound to try to recover them.

Then, even though the cowardice of his blacks was the real reason for the debacle, he considered it his duty to go to the help of any who had survived the attack. The Bambala wouldn't have slaughtered them all.

Once certain their victims were too terrorized to fight back, they would have begun taking prisoners.

And after an hour of pacing and fretting, he made up his mind. He wouldn't be able to live with himself if he didn't make a sincere attempt to free the surviving bearers and retake the records he had so painstakingly gathered.

Yet even as the resolve was formed, he felt himself doomed to failure. How could he, with a handful of pistol cartridges and an abysmal ignorance of the forest, hope to strike any kind of a blow against the savage Bambala?

Bob was surprised to see Abigale suddenly stride from the forest. He had thought her still asleep in the tree house. She leaned her spear against a tree, walked over and stirred the fire to life. "I left early," she said.

"I thought it wise to check on the Bambala." She knelt, placed four fresh sticks of wood in the flames. "The Bambala didn't turn back as I had hoped," she said abruptly. "They are searching for us now."

She loosened a leather pouch belted about her slim waist, laid it on a clean rock beside the fire.

Then, after selecting a long, pointed stick from a collection held in a large gourd, she reached in the pouch and drew out a freshly cleaned and dressed bird.

She held it up for him to see before she spitted it on the stick for cooking. "I thought these birds might please you for the morning meal," she said.

And so he would understand they were something special, she added, "I hunted for them quite awhile."

The girl utterly baffled Bob. She seemed to have dismissed the black warriors from her mind.

After learning those murderous devils were searching them out, how could she calmly go hunting and then come back to enjoy a leisurely meal. "The birds look wonderful," he said without enthusiasm. "But frankly, Abigale, shouldn't we be getting out of here instead of thinking of eating?"

"Leave?" she said, surprised. "This is my home!"

"You can't fight off a whole tribe," he told her.

Her eyes flashed. "I can cause them enough trouble to make them wish they hadn't come. I have done it before." "But they will come back, Abigale," he said calmly.

"And they will keep coming back until one day they will get you." She fitted the spitted birds onto the forked supports which held them over the fire. She stood up, brushed her hands. The merest shadow crossed her face.

"Death must come to each and every living creature someday," she declared. "I won't be frightened when my time comes."

Abigale spoke with the fatalism of those to whom danger is a constant companion. "Is there a way, Abigale," he asked abruptly, "for me to circle around these warriors and reach their village.

I'd imagine that most of the able-bodied men are now hunting for us. This may be the best opportunity to slip into their village and try to free the bearers who were captured.

If there are enough captured men they will help me, perhaps I can even recover my records."

Abigale turned in alarm. Though she'd talked calmly enough of death in regard to herself, she now exclaimed, "Are you trying to get yourself killed? You have to be a crazy man to speak of such a thing!" He blinked at her, taken aback by her reaction to his question.

She paced back and forth in front of him. "I haven't the least desire to get anywhere near that village," he admitted candidly, "but it's my responsibility to do it."

"Duty? I do not know this word!" She was like an aroused leopard, lithe and quick, with a wildness in her eyes. "I will not have you put yourself in danger. I will not have it, you understand!" Bob scratched his head and frowned.

He hadn't anticipated anything like this. "It's all right for you to play dangerous games with the Bambala, but not me. Is that it?"

She gave her long blond hair a savage toss. "I am different," she snapped.

"I am Abigale!" She reached him with quick steps, shook a finger in his face.

"Put this notion from your head. You are not to go anywhere near that kraal of dangos." "You saved my life, Abigale," he answered gently, "and I'm deeply grateful, but I'm not a new pet who will meekly do your bidding.

There are some things a man must do if he is to live with himself."

And he tried to explain to her then why he had to make a stab at helping the bearers and recovering the work of many months. "You owe those men nothing," she told him with harsh, feminine logic. "They did not value their freedom enough to fight for it.

As to this work you talk of, I do not understand about it too much, but it can't be important enough to lose your life over."

"Nevertheless, I must go," he said firmly.

She was very close to him. The changeful blue depths of her eyes softened, losing the storminess of a moment before. The warm, girl scent of her came up to Bob.

He watched the curve of her full, red lips. Her teeth were small and fine and white. He had never known any woman who stirred him as she did.

Suddenly the tight control he had exerted over himself snapped. Before he knew what he did, he reached his arms about her and pressed his mouth to hers.

The startled girl's eyes flew wide. She stiffened as though either to fight or run. But she let him draw her into his embrace, made no attempt to take her mouth from his.

Abruptly he released her, but he could not move away because she held him with the rigidness of her arms about his neck. "I'm sorry, Abigale," he muttered, "I shouldn't have done that.

I—I didn't mean to do it." He was embarrassed and angry with himself. "I only meant to tell you that though I wish I never had to see another Bambala, I have to go to their village." Abigale slid her arms from his neck and stepped back.

The strange, startled expression was still on her face. Her right hand came up to touch her mouth.

"Why did—what did you do?" she hesitated.

Bob scowled, briefly puzzled. Then he was more nervous than ever. Abigale had no knowledge what a kiss was. "I kissed you," he said. And then he didn't know what to say next.

"But why?" she demanded.

"Uh—well, I just couldn't help myself." His face reddened. "Among our people, when a man?" That didn't sound right. "It's a custom. It—it means—no, that's not what I want to say." He bumbled on in a growing confusion of unfinished sentences. "You mean," Abigale asked, "that among people with white skin it is like when a native man rubs noses with a girl?" "Yes," he granted uncomfortably.

He considered how swiftly feminine instinct had taken her to the heart of the matter. "I have seen them," she said thoughtfully. She touched her lips with her fingers. "This is a strange thing, this 'kiss,' very strange."

Then slowly, she smiled and nodded her head. "But it is far better than the natives' custom. I think our people must be very wise. First, there was the fire stick which kills at a distance, then the superior way of swimming, and now this matter."

"Then you aren't angry with me?" ventured Bob.

She contemplated him gravely.
"No," she said softly.
"I should like you to do it again, now when I wouldn't be so surprised."

Bob swallowed heavily. "Not now," he declared.
His breath came very fast. "No, not now."
He might have proved himself a sorry kind of man by making a mess of his expedition, he told himself, but he'd be damned if he was sorry enough to take advantage of Abigale innocence. She had saved his life. The least he could do was to behave himself.

Abigale sighed, tapped a forefinger against her teeth for a few moments. "Do not worry, Bob. If you must go through with this Bambala foolishness," she said in unexpected capitulation, "Abigale will make you a plan.
You sit here and rest. Fretting is not good for you." He was relieved to know she wasn't going to continue her opposition, though he didn't take seriously her easy assurance that she would provide a plan.

She was an unusual girl, but a foray such as he contemplated was rather out of a woman's line. He was amused by her swift shift from the role of a naive, young maiden to that of a wise elder mothering a child.

But later, after they had eaten, when he still hadn't laid hold of the vaguest notion of how to carry through his project, she calmly and confidently told him how the job could be done. She said, "This will work—if anything will.

I know the Bambala, how they think. And fortunately for us, only women and old men will be in the kraal."

Bob listened in amazement. Never in a thousand years would so unorthodox a scheme have occurred to him.

But, by George, it might work. It was bold and dangerous, yet properly executed it could so stun and frighten the tribesmen that he would have time to free his bearers and gather up his records before a hand was raised against him. Then his face suddenly fell.

Temba was the keystone of the whole plan, which he realized on second thought meant that Abigale was counting herself in on the raid.

"Oh, no," he cried.
"You're taking no part in this.

The plan won't do. I'm not risking your life on business that just concerns me." Abigale regarded the determined set of his jaw and smiled.

"You're mistaken," she said mildly. "The fight is entirely yours. I mean only to help you get ready for it and guide you to the village.

If I order it, Temba will do your bidding well enough to get you through." Bob subsided. "Well, that's different," he said.

"I won't have you running any more risks on my account. Look at the trouble I've already caused you."

Bob kept stressing that they need to leave the camp, throughout the day, But Abigale refused to be rushed. After several excursions into the forest to gather a peculiar range of roots, bulbs, and dank, yeasty growths, she'd settled down to combining a white, paste-like substance.

"Chimp and Sabot are keeping an eye on the Bambala," she told him. "They will let us know when the dangos get too close."

Bob did not agree with her trusting the two pets. And the fact that Chimp would get bored about every two hours and return to camp to see what Abigale was doing didn't help his nerves.

After the forest girl had chased the grumbling monkey back to his post for the 3rd time, she made a further confession to relieve Bob's tension.

"I laid enough false trails this morning to keep the Bambala busy until nightfall, unless they should get very lucky," she explained. "And scattered along each trail are some very small and unpleasant surprises to deter them from hurrying."

She did not go into detail about the surprises and he did not ask her to, for her grim tone brought crowding into his mind the variety of murderous traps he'd seen black men use in hunting: camouflaged pits, drawn bows released when a vine in the path was touched, small, poisoned bamboo splinters set in the ground, snares that would jerk a grown bushbuck eight feet in the air and break its neck, bent saplings that would hammer a lion into pulp.

But the revelation of how she had occupied the early morning shook him as badly as had the realization that Sabot, far more than a pet, was a deadly weapon she employed against her enemies.

When he looked at her now, he saw a young, mild, soft-voiced girl, anxious to please, quick to laugh.

He felt at ease with this girl. In truth, he felt pleasantly superior.

Then abruptly, she would shatter this mold into which he had fitted her, revealing by some action that she was more a sister to a tawny, dangerous lioness than the conventional being he tried to believe her to be.

How could he reconcile the shy, soft-mouthed girl he had held in his arms for a moment that morning with the Abigale who could meet and best the black warriors at their own savage game? It made him almost afraid of the girl.

You couldn't guess what really went on in that head of hers or predict how she would react in a given situation. How could he be sure she wouldn't turn on him, if he made a move that rubbed her the wrong way?

Abigale was too busy to notice any change in him. Not until late afternoon did she plug up with a stopper of wadded leaves the last of five large gourds of the thick, whitish liquid. She glanced at the low-lying sun and then came over to where Bob sat, then stretched out on her side on the ground beside him.

She smiled up at him, her head cushioned on her right arm. "The night ahead may be long," she said simply. "I will rest until Chimp comes. He would never forgive me for leaving him behind."

She closed her eyes, took a few slow, deep breaths and was immediately asleep.

Bob blinked in amazement. "That's not human," he told himself. "She even sleeps like a cat."

He set his jaw firmly and looked away into the forest. But in less than a minute his gaze had crept back to the sleeping form beside him.

He studied the way the long, blond hair tumbled about her face and shoulders, examined the long lashes lying heavy against her golden skin, watched with something more than scientific interest, the manner in which her red lips pouted in sleep.

The daylight was nearly gone when Bob realized with a start that Abigale eyes were open and that for some time she had been silently watching him. His confusion wasn't lessened when she said, "Chimp grows impatient with my laziness."

As though ear plugs had been drawn from his ears, he suddenly heard a monkey chattering and grumbling in the tree above them. How long the little devil had been there he didn't know, but apparently for a considerable period.

And though Chimp had made enough noise to rouse Abigale from sleep, Rob hadn't even been conscious of his presence. "It was nice to awaken and find you sitting beside me," she said, putting a hand on his arm.

"But I couldn't help but wonder what you were thinking that made you frown so."

He got up quickly, avoiding her gaze. "I was thinking of the raid," he lied. "Oh," she said quietly. And he had a queer feeling that she was smiling inwardly. While they waited for it to become full dark, they ate a light meal of fruit and nuts.

Then Abigale called Temba, tied the gourds on him so they wouldn't rattle or spill. Like the low, distant rumble of thunder, came the roar of a lion. After a brief interval, answering cries from widely separated points in the forest could be heard.

"The Bambala are close, but they won't do much more traveling tonight," said Abigale grimly. "That first roar was Sabot's victory cry, telling the forest he had made an easy kill. Every cat within hearing will head for that area. I think we can move safely now."

And so in the pitch blackness before the moon rose, Temba carried them along secret trails past the Bambala patrols. Bob, who had worried about the nervous, talkative Chimp going along with them, noticed that the monkey huddled in front of Abigale and never uttered a sound. He was about ready to believe that the forest girl's pets did understand what was going on.

It was after midnight when Abigale halted the elephant in a moonlit glade. "We'll do our work here," she said. "The kraal is within arrow shot."

She unfastened the gourds, detached two of them, and lowered the others carefully to the ground. "I'll paint his head and back," she told Bob. "You take care of his legs and stomach."

A half-hour later the patient elephant had been smeared completely over with the thick, white liquid brewed by Abigale. But in the darkness, the liquid revealed a property not discernible during daylight. It glowed with an eerie, phosphorescent light.

Bob stood off and looked at Temba. "By Harry," he exclaimed, "he's the most unearthly-looking sight I ever hope to see. And that hazy, bluish glow makes him look twice as big as he is.

A creature like that looming out of the night would frighten anyone." "The Abama witch woman who brought me up used it in her magic," explained Abigale. "I often helped her gather the materials and mix it."

Bob looked at his hands, glowing with light from the mixture he had smeared over the elephant. "I believe it may work," he excitedly declared, "if the Bambala are as superstitious as you say." "Let us hope so," the girl said quietly.

"There will be danger enough at best." Abigale had picked up the vine rope which had been used to tie the gourds on Temba. As she talked, she idly toyed with it, forming loose coils on the ground with one end, twisting and gathering the other end in an odd pattern.

"Well, this finishes your part of the job, anyway," said Bob. "You've been wonderful to help me." He tried to tell her how grateful he was, but he seemed suddenly clumsy with words and his voice took on an unnatural brusqueness.

He finished lamely by saying, "I'd better paint myself up now. And then as soon as you get me started off on Temba, I want you to get away from here—and stay away. You've taken too many chances on my account already." Abigale didn't look at him.

She kept her head down, her fingers nervously working with the rope. "Yes, Bob," she said.

She seemed small and feminine and terribly forlorn in the moonlight. The sight of her caught Bob's heart and twisted it. He had been a rotten, miserable heel to think of her as he had that afternoon. He couldn't leave her this way.

He had to take her in his arms, tell her how he felt about her. He took two steps towards her. "Abigale," he said hoarsely, "before I go—"As though her mind had been turned inward and she hadn't heard him, she suddenly interrupted.

"The paint, Bob—it must be dry before you mount Temba. Hold out your hands and let me see if it is drying properly."

Her taut, businesslike tone, so out of harmony with the mood that had swept over him, stopped Bob in his tracks. Almost angrily, he shoved out his hands for her inspection. As to what happened next, he was to try many times afterwards to recall exactly how it did occur. But he was never to be entirely certain about any of it.

Abigale leaned as though to inspect his hands. The next thing he knew the vine rope she had been idly fingering snapped about his wrists. "What the devil?" he exclaimed.

Before he could realize what she was about, Abigale leaped backwards, the rope running through her hands with the speed of a striking snake. Then she flipped the rope, gave a powerful tug—and Bob's feet shot from under him.

One end of the vine was lashed about his wrists, the other about his ankles.

There had been careful planning behind all her nonchalant handling of the rope while they talked. The loops she had thrown on the ground with seeming carelessness were those she flicked upward to lash his ankles, send him crashing to the ground.

Despite the stunning force of the fall he took, Bob lashed out wildly, trying to break free. After darting in to snatch his pistol from its holster, Abigale stood a safe distance away, watching him struggle.

He fought like a maddened beast, his sanity momentarily splintered by the terrible shock of her treachery.

But the bonds held, and at last he lay gasping, his muscles trembling from the violence of his efforts.

Only then did he look at her, letting the bitter acid of his wrath spill out in words. "And to think I believed in you, trusted you," he snarled. "I should have known you'd turn on me like an animal if it were to your advantage."

His mouth was a vicious slit, his eyes narrow pools of hate. His gun made a dull thump as she dropped it at her feet.

"You fooled me, though," continued Bob.

"I swallowed all your hocus-pocus, never suspecting that you'd use me to buy your own safety. Very clever! You hand me over to the

Bambala and thereby buy them off of your own trail. They were getting too close for comfort.

And you got to worrying that if I did raid their kraal and did some damage, they'd never forgive you for helping me."

Abigale smoothed her hands nervously over her midriff, her face expressionless except for the eyes which seemed to glow in the night. Finally, her right hand slid to the knife riding the curve of her hip. The blade gleamed coldly as she lifted it from the sheath.

CHAPTER SIX

******

Bob was abruptly still as he saw the bared steel in the forest girl's hand. Then with withering contempt, he said, "Don't lose your head, my precious.

The Bambala won't pay as much for me dead as they will alive. They, too, enjoy the pleasure of killing!" A deep, pained frown cut Abigale forehead. She had foreseen everything in her planning except Bob's reaction.

The awful bitterness of his words took her by surprise.

"Yes, I play a hard trick on you," she said evenly. "But I play it to save your life, not take it away." She turned her back on him. The gray trunk of a dead tree stood at the edge of the clearing some thirty paces in front of her.

She covered half the distance to the tree with quick steps. Then Abigale lifted the knife, sent it glittering through the air to drive point-first into the dead wood. Bob had lifted himself with difficulty to a sitting position.

He watched her fling the knife into the tree and hurry back to where Temba waited.

"What did you mean about saving my life?" he demanded.

She picked up the remaining half-gourd of phosphorescent paint, literally poured it over her head and shoulders, saving back enough to douse the protesting Chimp.

Then she painted both her spear and bow. "I meant I am going in your place!" she snapped, rapidly smearing the paint evenly over her.

"Foolish one, Temba would never take your orders, and besides, I know far more about handling the Bambala than you do."

He stared at her aghast as she signaled Temba to lift Chimp and her to his back. "You intended this from the beginning?" "Of course," she said, "if your men and packs can be wrested from the Bambala, I will do it.

If I fail, then you will still be able to save yourself."

"No!" he burst out indignantly. "I won't allow it!"

He was working clumsily with his fingers to loosen the bonds on his ankles. Since Abigale had tied his hands in front of him, he had no trouble reaching his feet. "I tied you so you'd have to allow it," she said calmly. "And don't waste your strength trying to undo those knots. You'll need my knife to get free. By the time you work your way over to that tree and get it loose, it will be too late for you to interfere at the kraal."

Abigale lifted her pet monkey and dropped him to the ground. "However, on second thought I'll leave Chimp to help take care of you. The noise he's making would work me harm, but his voice and looks should protect you from anything less than a rhino."

She tried to force a light-hearted gayety into her tone, but the attempt wasn't wholly successful. "I go now!" she said abruptly, lifting her spear in an odd, quick salute.

Then Temba was moving past Bob, bearing Abigale into the forest. He pleaded with her not to go, nearer in his utter helplessness to tears than at any time since his early childhood. Abigale, sitting ramrod straight, didn't look back.

As the dark, green foliage closed behind her, Bob's voice trailed away brokenly.

He thought of things he had said to her in anger and was ashamed and miserable.

She was going into that village for him and only because of him. He had called her an animal, immediately attributing the basest motives to her. He remembered the hurt, surprised look on her face as she heard his accusations. Yet she hadn't even rebuked him.

In that moment, the certainty crystallized in him that he would never see Abigale again. She was riding to her death!

In one writhing effort, Bob heaved himself to his feet. He had to get free and catch her. He reeled, his legs so tightly bound he couldn't balance himself.

To keep from falling, he started hopping forward, each clumsy hop swifter and more desperate than the preceding one. But his convulsive efforts to regain his equilibrium were doomed to failure. He got no more than five yards before he crashed heavily to the hard earth.

The fall knocked the breath from him, yet he immediately fought to his elbows and knees.

He heard a weird gibberish sounding right at his shoulder. He jerked his heel around and saw Chimp crouched on hands and knees beside him.

The monkey, his eerily glowing face seemingly wreathed with diabolical delight, was trying to assume the same position as, Bob.

The distraught man's temper exploded. "I'll teach you to mock me," he shouted. And he reared up on his knees, lifting his bound arms to knock the monkey rolling.

But Chimp divined his purpose instantly. With an alarmed screech, the monkey bounded backwards and fled off across the clearing like some small, incandescent demon. Bob shook his knotted fists in futile, senseless rage.

Chimp literally flew over the ground, his little head twisting right and left in search of a safe refuge. The gray outlines of the dead tree caught his attention as it had Abigale when she looked for a place to plant the knife.

The monkey headed for the tree. He scrambled up the trunk in mad haste, shooting past the knife to reach the bare lower limbs. Not until then did he pause to look back. His staccato outburst revealed surprise that the man hadn't moved.

He fell silent, considering the matter. Then deciding he was quite safe, his whole manner changed and he began climbing slowly down the tree, grandly announcing his outrage at being put upon like a common fellow.

When Chimp reached the knife, he suddenly stopped his tirade. He recognized the scent of his beloved mistress. He gave a delighted cry and tugged the knife free. He beamed on the weapon. It was Abigale.

He would return it to Abigale and she would be pleased with him. She was always very proud of him when he returned some belonging of hers that he found. In fact, if the truth were known, he often stole her belongings so he might return them and have her pleased with him.

His run-in with Bob had slipped as completely out of Chimp's erratic little mind as had his memory that Abigale was gone. His head did not trouble itself very often to try to hold more than one opinion at a time.

He dropped from the tree and scampered happily back toward Bob. He was within three yards of the man when he realized that Abigale was nowhere in sight. Chimp was too busy been angry about the white paint being poured on him to pay any attention to Abigale departure, and after that, Bob's antics had so engrossed him that he did not realize he'd been deserted.

All at once it was borne in on him that his protector was gone and that the terrible night so feared by the tree people kept him from finding her. Chimp was frightened.

He looked around at the trees in the dark, envisioning fearful enemies staring at him. Bob had no notion what went on in Chimp's mercurial head. The white man crouched on his knees, his breath coming in hard gasps.

The monkey had the knife. That was all that mattered.

From the second Chimp had pulled the knife from the tree and started back toward him, Bob had been afraid to move or speak. He had to get the weapon from the little devil.

But how? After the way he had treated the monkey, a small step or word from him would likely send Chimp fleeing into the forest. He wet his lips nervously, "Here Chimp! Good little boy, give me the knife." The words came out of his mouth like a prayer. "Nice boy. I won't hurt you."

Chimp, who'd crouched down into a little glowing knot, slowly lifted his head and gave the white man a mournful stare. He then shivered and ducked his face. Bob kept talking in the mellow, wheedling tone.

The monkey would not budge. Bob edged forward a couple of inches and gathered his nerve. Chimp edged backwards an equal distance without lifting his head.

Bob groaned. He'd never get the knife, never in the world. The little fool understood and obeyed every word Abigale spoke, yet at this moment, when so much depended on it, he wouldn't heed a single thing Bob said to him. And then abruptly, Bob realized that in his excitement, he had been speaking in English.

With his voice trembling with excitement, he switched to the Bambala tongue.

Chimp straightened, cocking his head to listen. He seemed to feel better immediately. He began to chatter and moved cautiously in towards the man. Bob was careful to make no sudden moves.

Not until the monkey had snuggled against him did he gently reach for the knife. To his relief, Chimp seemed actually happy to give the weapon up. Bob's face and hands were bathed with sweat and he was shaking as he cut away his rope bonds.

He shoved the knife under his belt, ran to where Abigale had dropped his pistol. Then gun in hand, he raced toward the point where the forest girl had left the clearing, praying that he would be able to follow her in the dark.

He was in luck for once. Temba had left a clear trail where he had forced his way through

the undergrowth, and within a distance of
twenty yards, Bob hit a broad trail, from the
angle at which the elephant had slanted into the
trail, there was no doubting the direction
Abigale had taken.

As he started to run, a hysterical jabbering
broke out behind him. Chimp, refusing to be
abandoned, came rocketing out of the
underbrush and in an amazing leap, fastened
himself on Bob's back.

He hugged himself against the white man so
tightly, his small heart pounding with fright
that Bob couldn't bring himself to throw him
off.

"All right," growled Bob. "You can play Old
Man of the Sea until we come in sight of the
kraal. Then you're going back on your own!"
And with that, he sprinted on down the trail
with redoubled effort.

After Abigale left Bob tied in the clearing, she
turned her whole mind to the task ahead of her.
By the time she reached the Bambala kraal, the
final details of her plan were perfected.

The walled village lay silent and sleeping in
the waning moonlight. If there were sentries
posted, they rested listlessly out of sight, lulled
by the long, monotonous hours of early
morning.

The campfires had died to ash-whitened coals. Abigale had carefully selected this as the most propitious time for her raid.

The forest girl urged Temba straight up to the big main gate. In these first few moments, boldness would be her most valuable weapon.

When the elephant slowed his pace before the gate, not yet understanding what was expected of him, Abigale drummed her heels behind his ears, drove him head-on against the massive barrier.

"Forwards, O Mightiest of Elephants," she encouraged him. "Let these jackals know your strength." There was a splintering impact. For a few seconds, the bull mammoth seemed to hesitate.

Then the huge gate snapped free of hinges and cross bars, fell inward with a powerful crash that.

And Temba, exhilarated from the exploit, lifted his trunk and trumpeted in ear- splitting challenge to all comers as he carried his mistress into the kraal. Two guards who were dozing beside the gate on a catwalk, crouched frozen on their knees.

Their eyes gleamed from the darkness like great, ring-shaped bulbs as they stared at the ghostly apparition sweeping into the kraal.

"Tremble, you curs," cried Abigale, gesturing toward them with her spear, "For the curse of doom is on you! I, who am the servant of Gimshai, dread god of death, proclaim this doom on Bambala!"

Of all the fearsome forest deities, the all-powerful Gimshai struck the greatest terror into the hearts of black men.

And as every native knew, Gimshai's servants appeared in a thousand, thousand different forms, struck at their chosen victims in ways that were unnumbered.

The terror of one of the guards was so great that after hearing Abigale words he toppled forward senseless on the platform. Another man, quaking in every muscle, jerked upright on the platform.

Tedious, nerve-splitting screams ripped from his throat.

He plunged off the catwalk, hit on the ground with bone-breaking force. But terror numb any physical hurt he endured was, and he was on his feet and running with great speed, streaking down the main way of the kraal.

The guards' screams ripped the blanket of sleep from the entire village. Commands, shouts, the sound of running feet boiled up from the dark clusters of huts.

Confused women and men poured from narrow, skin-hung doorways.

Abigale rode in the middle of the unexpectedly aroused ant-heap. She went straight down the main way of the village, looking neither to left nor right, the one completely calm, collected person in all that howling throng.

The mammoth elephant and Abigale seemed enveloped in a swirling, blue-white haze of light.

Temba looked even more massive than he actually was, and the din of his steady trumpeting, inspired by the smell of the Bambala and all the excitement, was indeed like the sound of doom. As the blacks, crowding outside to know the reason for the disruption, saw that white, statue-like figure that was Abigale, the furor that was loud died away like a fading echo.

A low, fearful moan that could have been the keening of the wind aver a wasteland swept back and back through the massing natives.

Then Abigale voice, brutal and savage, was heard.

"From the Black Hole of Death, from the Skull-Throne of the Terrible God himself, I bring you the curse of Gimshai."

Look at me, O members of a jackal-tribe!
Look at me and tremble, for I'm the Clawed
Hand of Gimshai; I'm the Net of the Eater of
Souls; I'm the Sword of the God of Death." Her
words drove into the Bambala's minds like
poisoned darts.

Had she rehearsed her speech to Bob Reilly
he would have thought it was nonsense and
suicidal. But Abigale knew the best way to
open the floodgates of fear in her audience.

The entire existence of these wild and
primitive natives was a web of superstition.
Any strange or unexplained phenomena they
attributed to gods or demons. And their over-
active imaginations seized on every untoward
event and embroidered it with supernatural
significance.

Even now as they gazed at the strange, chalk-
white she-demon, their imaginations swiftly
added a variety of details to what they thought
they saw. There were some who saw in the
whiteness of her face the clear outlines of a
deaths head.

Others saw her long hair, stiffly encrusted
with white liquid, as a mass of pale squirming
snakes. Some would say afterwards her eyes
were hollow black sockets, others that they
were red coals of fire.

It would be said that the spear in her hand squirmed and wriggled like a living thing, that the eerie, elephant-like apparition she rode was no more than a mist through which one could see, that rivulets of cold flame ran outward along the ground where the creature's feet were placed.

Abigale audience was especially impressionable on this night when practically the whole of its fighting strength was absent. Excited by their triumph of the previous day, every warrior eagerly had sought to join the hunt for Bob Reilly and the forest girl.

Left behind in the kraal were the untried youths, the men too old or sick for trekking, and the easily frightened mass of women and children.

Abigale had counted on the absence of the real fighting men as a major help in the carrying out of her colossal bluff.

Now as she heard the whimpering of the women, saw the crowd edge backward away from her, she boldly rode into the central clearing, abandoning any hope of retreat.

She knew the crowd would mass around the open space, and if she were found out, that wall of humanity would prevent her from ever reaching the gate alive.

After the habit of the Bambala, both the prisoners and the loot gained in their attack on Bob's safari were kept on display in the clearing. The miserable bearers were crowded into a foul, make-shift pen like animals, and stacked near the enclosure were the packs they once had carried.

The great feast and the ceremony of dividing the spoils which always followed a battle triumph were being delayed until Bob and Abigale were captured. Abigale headed the elephant toward the pen, wanting to free the prisoners and march them out of the kraal before the stunned tribesmen could collect their wits.

But suddenly two of the large cooking fires in the clearing flickered into life. Yellow tongues of flame reached along the edges of the dry wood which had been thrown hastily on the coals.

Abigale understood then the purpose of the commands that had sounded in the first uproar of her entrance, for revealed in the mounting light was a hollow square of armed guards grouped about two men, the two most important men in the tribe.

One was Boboli, the immensely fat chieftain of the Bambala, a brutal, self-indulgent tyrant. The other was Nyag-Nyag, a tall, thin, one-eyed man with a hatchet face and the hunched posture of a crouching weasel.

Nyag-Nyag was the Bambala witch doctor, and more than any other member of the tribe, he had reason to hate Abigale, for time and again the most potent magic he could make against her had proved ineffectual.

CHAPTER SEVEN

******

A bigale instantly was disturbed when she saw the two tribal leaders with the ranks of hard-bitten guards ranged about them. She certainly hadn't counted on their presence. Improvising to meet this unexpected danger, she hastily changed her plans and halted Temba.

Gesturing contemptuously with her spear, she cried, "Hai! So now I look upon the two chief jackals!" The elephantine Boboli clearly was more shaken by her ghostly appearance than the witch doctor.

"Why—why—have you come here?" he asked weakly.

Abigale was silent for long, ominous moments. Then like the crack of a whip her voice lashed him. "I come to take your soul to ever-lasting torment! Even now, Gimshai wrathfully awaits your coming!"

The mammoth chieftain stumbled back a step, his great belly quivering. The harsh confidence with which she spoke turned his blood to ice. "There is some terrible mistake," he quavered. "Never by word or deed have I shown disrespect for Gimshai! Aaiiee, he is the greatest of gods! In all the forest, no one has sent him more souls than Boboli."

"It's too late to lie," Abigale said grimly. "You honor but one god, N'Koto, god of war, and it is he who has led you to your downfall. Two suns ago you made a cowardly attack upon the safari of one who holds the special favor of Gimshai.

The Taker of Souls reached out his hand and saved this white man, saying for the destruction you had wrought you would pay with your life. And so I have come to exact payment!"

Boboli seemed to be choking. His eyes stood out like round, red marbles. Poisoned by a lifetime of superstition, he felt that already the life-force was being sucked from his body, that the fluttering in his throat was his soul struggling to escape.

"Talk to her! Appease her!" he gasped to the witch doctor. "You know more of gods and demons than I do. Promise anything — anything — if she will let me be."

With his one good eye, the witch doctor had been glaring at Abigale. He was not as naive as Boboli, nor as superstitious as the other tribesmen. He had practiced too much trickery and deceit, pawned off too much humbug as magic, to be taken in easily by Abigale tricks.

He sensed something familiar in this ghostly intruder, noted also how she sought to keep back out of the firelight. It seemed to him that every time an especially high leap of the flames lighted her mount that its eerie blue-white glow disappeared.

Yet because he was both a cunning man and a coward, Nyag-Nyag proceeded with care. He pushed through the ranks of warriors, picked a blazing stick from the fire.

He lifted the torch high as though to clearly light himself for Abigale eyes. "Hear me, O One Who Walks the Night," he said in a false, fawning voice. "I make no plea for my worthless, unimportant self, but I do plead for the noble Boboli."

He edged nearer to Temba as he talked, narrowly watching the effect of the torchlight on the elephant's glowing whiteness.

"Never would Boboli knowingly offend the dread Taker of Souls," he continued. "If a wrong has been done by Boboli, he stands ready to make any gifts, offering or sacrifices the god decrees. Intercede for us, O Great One, and the Bambala will honor you endlessly.

Help us to right our unmeant wrong! You have only to speak." Relief surged through Abigale as she listened to Nyag-Nyag's abject beseeching. The feeling that she had triumphed lessened her wariness, so that she failed to divine the witch doctor's purpose in coming so near.

"Gimshai is merciful, as are his servants," she said haughtily. "If you have the courage to accompany me into the Black Hole of Death to plead your case before the god himself, you may do so—remembering that if you fail, there can be no return." Nyag-Nyag seemed to debate before muttering, "I have the courage." Abigale stared at him.

"But you must approach Gimshai with clean hands." She gestured at the imprisoned bearers and stacked loot. "You must give up the spoils of your cowardly attack. You must free the bearers and give them back their arms and you must furnish men to carry these packs to their destination."

The huge-bellied chieftain, who had been bathed in sweat as he waited for Abigale answer, literally shouted his acceptance of her terms.

He was concerned with his own safety only, and cared not a whit that he might be sending a large group of his followers to their death.

"All shall be as you say!" Boboli shouted hoarsely, not wanting to give the witch doctor time to back out of his bargain.

He then turned to his guards in the exact same frantic haste, shouting, "Release the prisoners! Assemble men enough to take the packs! Immediately, you curs!"

But as the tribal chief spoke, Nyag-Nyag sprang back Away from Temba, swirling the torch above his head.

"No!" he roared. "Let no man move."

BOBOLI was so shocked that it took him a minute to find his voice. His body quivered with rage at this treachery. "I'm chieftain here," he muttered. "You are an idiot, Boboli," snarled the witch doctor, "as blind and ignorant as all these others!"

It was in Nyag-Nyag's mind that after tonight he would never again have to bend his knee to the fat chieftain.

What he was about to do would make Boboli a laughingstock at the same time that it boost his reputation as a sorcerer.

"Because I amuse myself by toying with this impostor," the witch doctor said, pointing his finger at Abigale, "do not take my acting seriously. She's no devil, no servant of Gimshai."

"What exactly are you saying?" squeaked the chieftain, seeing his odds of redemption being shattered before his eyes.

Nyag-Nyag laughed, baring his bright yellow teeth. "I am saying this supposed demon is just Tioto Nomi, the forest Girl.

I am saying it requires more than kid's tricks to deceive the forest's greatest sorcerer."

Dismay had wrenched Abigale upright. But Abigale's reaction was no distinct from that which shook Boboli's tribesmen. The witch doctor's words had exploded with the violence of a thunderbolt.

"You madman!" wailed Boboli. "You'd get us all killed. You know as well as I that our warriors are pursuing Tioto Nomi far across the forest." Nyag-Nyag had backed close to the guards.

He threw away the torch in his hand, took a shield and a spear from one of the blacks. He then ran out into the open space between the warriors and Abigale. "Watch this test, my simple Boboli," he sneered. "And you need not faint from terror, as the risk falls on me alone."

His whole manner was supremely confident. "A thousand shields, would not protect me from a servant of Gimshai, because such a servant would have the ability to kill with a glance—a sign—a thought."

The ugly laughter bubbled from his lips again. After tonight, his name would ring through the forest.

"But one shield is protection enough against Tioto Nomi," he said, "because her only weapon is her spear.

She has no magic powers. Watch while I prove it! And stand ready, guards, to strike her down when she betrays herself by trying to use her one, puny weapon."

Abigale sat stupefied, a knot of panic growing and spreading in her breast. The cunning, one-eyed dango had trapped her. She sought in futile desperation for some means of escape, knowing full well that the game was played out.

Nyag-Nyag was leaping and dancing in front of her, always careful to protect himself behind the thick, heavy shield of rhino hide. "Quickly, Tioto Nomi," he taunted, "loose your terrible magic. Kill me with a look! Kill me with a thought!"

A stifling hush gripped the kraal. In the shadows around the central clearing, black men crouched, afraid to breathe.

Boboli leaned forward, his face like gray paste, his mouth hanging loosely open.

"Come, O Would-be Demon," the prancing wizard jeered, "I wait for you to strike.

Why do you hesitate? You try my patience, make me weary of this farce."

Abigale mouth was dust-dry. The death she had sought to save Bob Reilly from was to be hers. And now he was to be lost to her finally and forever.

As inauspicious mumbling disturbed the blacks who were watching. Nyag-Nyag's mockery was taking its effect. The guards were already moving forward, their hands gripping their spears.

Abigale own spear arm tensed. Her bluff was completed. At least, she would take some of them. She gritted her teeth, prepared to send Temba charging into the guards.

Nyag-Nyag's smirking laughter echoed. "Hear me, Tioto Nomi," he shrilled. "I spit on your fathers and on you! What greater insult can one give?" His prancing and his high pitched shouts were too much for Temba. The enormous bull elephant trumpeted with earsplitting violence and lifted his trunk. The very air shivered with the raging sound.

Nyag-Nyag looked up startled. Then something strange happen. The hatchet- faced sorcerer gave a queer backward jump as though he had been struck a powerful blow. His face twisted in anguish and he staggered. He let the spear drop from his fingers, and the weight of the shield slowly drew his left arm down to his side.

His muscles that were stringy started twitching and jerking. His single eye bulged with terror. Then his long slender legs started to buckle. All at once his mouth strained wide and a great wash of blood rushed from his lips.

That was the end. Nyag-Nyag toppled forward on his face and lay still. Temba fell silent at that same moment. It was unbelievable that a native kraal could be so still.

And in that profound hush, you could feel terror sweep like a black wind over the stunned natives. Abigale was as shocked as the tribesmen. She stared blankly at the dead sorcerer. Abigale hadn't moved a muscle to harm him, yet there lay the hated Nyag-Nyag, stiffening in death.

What kind of miracle was this? What unseen power had reached out in her hour of need to strike down that human dango? But, Abigale had no time to think about that mystery. Boboli's hysterical shrill cry jolted her alert. The fat tribal chief had fallen to his knees and was begging for his life, not to blame him for NyagNyag's profanities. Tribesmen all about the clearing were cringing in hopeless terror.

They thought she had slain the wizard!

Abigale went quickly to take advantage of the situation. Though so upset herself that she could hardly keep her voice from trembling, she sternly repeated the demands she had made before. And this time the guards freed the prisoners immediately and Boboli's disarmed guards loaded themselves down with all the stolen packs with no thought of opposing Abigale.

Then the Boboli collapsed in a blubbering heap, but Abigale wasted no time and delegated four of the bearers to prod him using their spears. The remaining bearers she placed along both sides of the pack-laden Bambala.

"Now trek," she yelled. "And any man who causes trouble will join Nyag-Nyag in his ever-lasting torment." The threat sent the column through the kraal at a stumbling trot. All thoughts of resistance was gone from the Bambala.

The natives pressed their faces in the dirt, afraid to look at her as she urged Temba to go after the bearers.

Once outside the kraal, she forged to the head of the column, guiding it back toward the trail where she'd left Bob Reilly.

But before she had gone very far, she heard a frantic chattering, saw an eerie, glowing small figure come skittering down the dim trail toward her.

"Chimp!" she shouted in surprise, and with a quick command, she had the elephant swing the small monkey up beside her.

Chimp bounded into her arms, fairly sputtering with delight at finding his mistress again. Then Abigale keen ears heard another sound.

She looked up to see Bob advancing out of the darkness. Her initial thought was that he might still be angry at her.

But there was unutterable relief, not anger, in his voice as he exclaimed, "Thank heavens you're out of that place at last! You were crazy to take such a chance, but it was the most wonderful thing I've ever seen."

"You mean you saw what went on in the kraal?" she asked, surprised. "I not only saw —

thanks to Chimp, not you," he said, "but I took a small part in the proceedings. I'll frankly admit that I could never have pulled off the bluff you did."

He told her then how when he reached the kraal the witch doctor had just begun to taunt her.

Since the natives were all concentrated in the center of the village, he was able to enter the gate unobserved, He had sneaked close to the clearing, climbed up on a pile of wood stacked beside a hut.

With his pistol, he had blasted Nyag-Nyag. The sound of the shot had been covered by Temba's wrathful trumpeting.

And the unholy fear that had struck into the Bambala when they saw their witch doctor die, had kept them from suspecting that any hand but Gimshai's had slain Nyag-Nyag.

"So you were the one who saved me," she said wonderingly.

Bob laughed. "I believe I could say the same for you."

They were a mile further down the trail and the false dawn was graying the sky when Abigale halted the elephant.

Bob sat behind her on the forest giant's back.

"What do we do now?" he asked.

She gave him a long, searching look.

"You will take Boboli and his guards with you and see that they are punished. You'll have no more trouble with the Bambala, so you can easily reach white man's country with your records."

"You—you—aren't going out with me?" Bob was surprised and confused. "This is my own land," she said, gesturing toward the dark forest with her hand.

"There are many things I can do to make it a better land. I have found myself tonight, as the old witch woman once prophesied I would."

Her head lifted and she looked up at the brightening sky.

"But you can't stay here, a lone girl," said Bob.

"I've grown very fond of you, Abigale. I want you to go with me. I thought that you and I?" "Even if I wished it," she interrupted him gently, "I could not go with you. I am a priestess and more to the Abamas.

They have been awaiting the day when I would be ready to lead them. And now I am ready. It would mean your certain death if you tried to take me away." And so it was that a frowning, unhappy man a few minutes later watched Abigale ride away alone toward the Abama kraal.

He stood there with the soft warmth of her good-bye kiss on his lips, vowing that Abama warriors or not, he would be back as soon as his trek to the coast was finished.